Stinky Socks

by Justine Korman
illustrated by Dan Regan

little rainl

Troll Associates

Coach Cramp always says, "Wash your gym socks, boys. If you don't, they'll come to life."

No one believes him, except me. Because once it really happened!

My gym socks were dirty. But I kept forgetting to bring them home.

Then they smelled so bad, I didn't *want* to bring them home. I was afraid my socks would stink up the school bus.

Instead, I brought in a new pair of socks. I left the old ones in the back of my gym locker. They smelled so rotten, I couldn't bring myself to touch them. I figured I would leave them there until the end of the year. And then next year I would get a new gym locker.

I figured wrong!

One day I opened my locker and my old socks jumped out!

"Ughh! What's that smell?" asked Stevie.

"Whose socks are those?" Matt the Rat wanted to know.

Soon all the boys were pointing at my stinky socks. Those socks were running around the locker room!

I guess they were pretty happy to be out. I guess they were tired of being left all alone in the locker doing nothing. I guess I'm crazy if I'm trying to figure out what a pair of socks is feeling.

Only those were no ordinary socks!

I didn't want anyone to know the stinky gym socks were mine. So I ran out of the locker room. But the socks followed me.

Everyone in the hall held their noses. They stared at the socks hopping after me wherever I went.

I felt like Mary with her little lamb. Only I had a pair of stinky gym socks!

"Stay!" I shouted.
But the socks wouldn't stay.
"Go home!" I cried.
That didn't work, either.
"Heel!" I yelled.

The socks did. *Heel* was the only command they obeyed.

In fact, those stinky socks stayed on my heels day after day!

The socks followed me home from school.
They followed me on my paper route.

Those stinky socks even went to my piano lesson. They smelled so bad, Mrs. Forte fainted. That was the shortest piano lesson I ever had!

And that was the only good thing those socks did.

Then those stinky socks ruined my sleep-out.
The other scouts made me move my tent to the
next hill.

Even the mosquitoes didn't want to sleep near my socks!

I tried to wash those stinky gym socks. But they jumped right out of the washing machine.

All I wanted was for my life to get back to normal.

I tried locking my stinky gym socks in a closet.

But those socks were on their toes! They slipped out under the door.

"Those stinky socks follow you everywhere!"
Stevie complained. "They'll go anywhere you go!"

And that gave me an idea. It was just crazy
enough to work. In a flash I was on my feet and
ready to try.

I left the park with the stinky socks right behind me.

I ran through town.

Finally, I got to Cooper's Car Wash. I paid the clerk five dollars.

I looked down. The stinky socks were right by my side.

We ran through the soap.

We ran
through the
brushes.

We ran through the rinse.

By the time we reached the wax, the stinky socks had stopped running.

I picked the wet socks off the ground.

They weren't alive anymore. They were just ordinary gym socks.

Hooray!
I took the socks home. I washed them two more times, just in case.

Now when Coach Cramp says, "Remember to wash your gym socks, boys," you can bet your bunions I do!

I wash my gym shorts, too. And sometimes I even wash my gym sneakers—because you can never be too careful!